Little White Dog

Little White Dog

Laura Godwin

Illustrated by Dan Yaccarino

SCHOLASTIC INC.

New York   Toronto   London   Auckland   Sydney   Mexico City   New Delhi   Hong Kong

ISBN: 0-439-06480-5

Published by Scholastic Inc.,
555 Broadway, New York, NY 10012,
by arrangement with Hyperion Books for Children.
SCHOLASTIC and associated logos are trademarks
and/or registered trademarks of Scholastic Inc.

12 11 10 9 8 7 6 5 4 3 2   1 2 3 4/0

Printed in the U.S.A.   14

First Scholastic printing, January 1999

This book is set in 48-point and 64-point Eras Demi.
The artwork for each picture was prepared
using gouache on Arches watercolor paper

For Rachel
—L. G.

For Ralph
—D. Y.

Little White Dog in the snow, snow's so white

where did you go?

Little Blue Bird
in the sky,
sky's so blue

where did you fly?

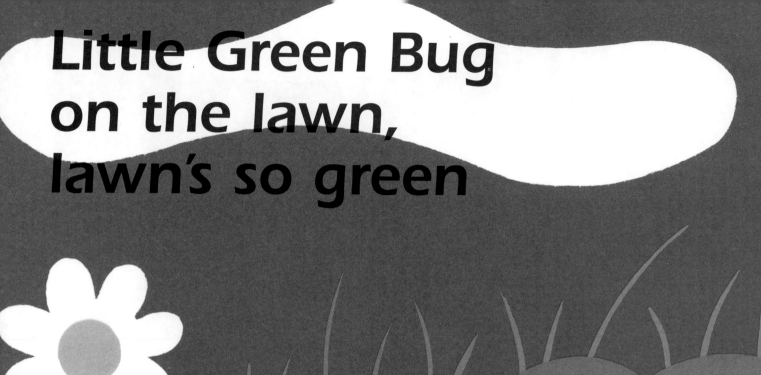

Little Green Bug
on the lawn,
lawn's so green

where have you gone?

Little Brown Horse
on the track,
track's so brown

won't you come back?

Little Yellow Chick
in the hay,
hay's so yellow

won't you *stay?*

Little Black Cat
in the night,
night's so black—

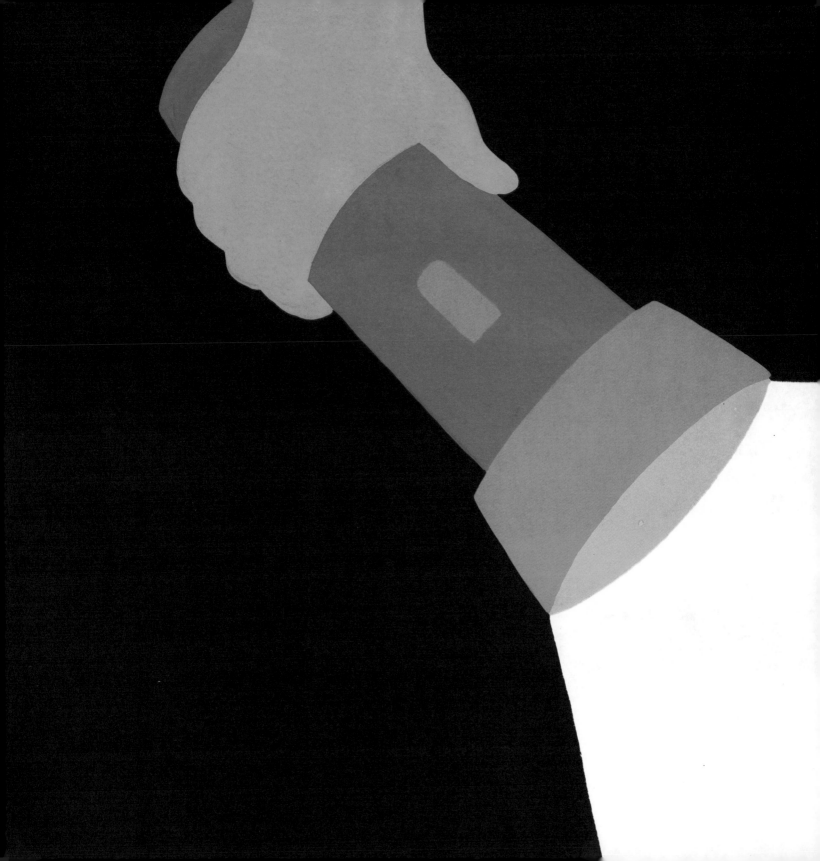

TURN ON THE LIGHT!

Turn on the light and you will find . . .

Little Black Cat,
who went to find . . .

**Little Yellow Chick,
who went to find . . .**

Little Brown Horse,
who went to find . . .

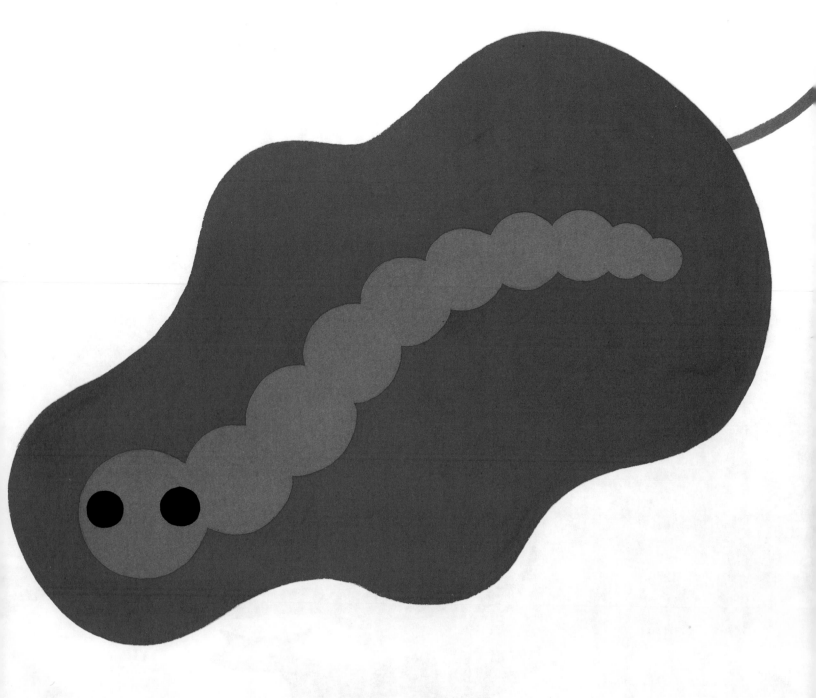

**Little Green Bug,
who went to find . . .**

Little Blue Bird,
who went to find . . .

Little White Dog
in the snow.

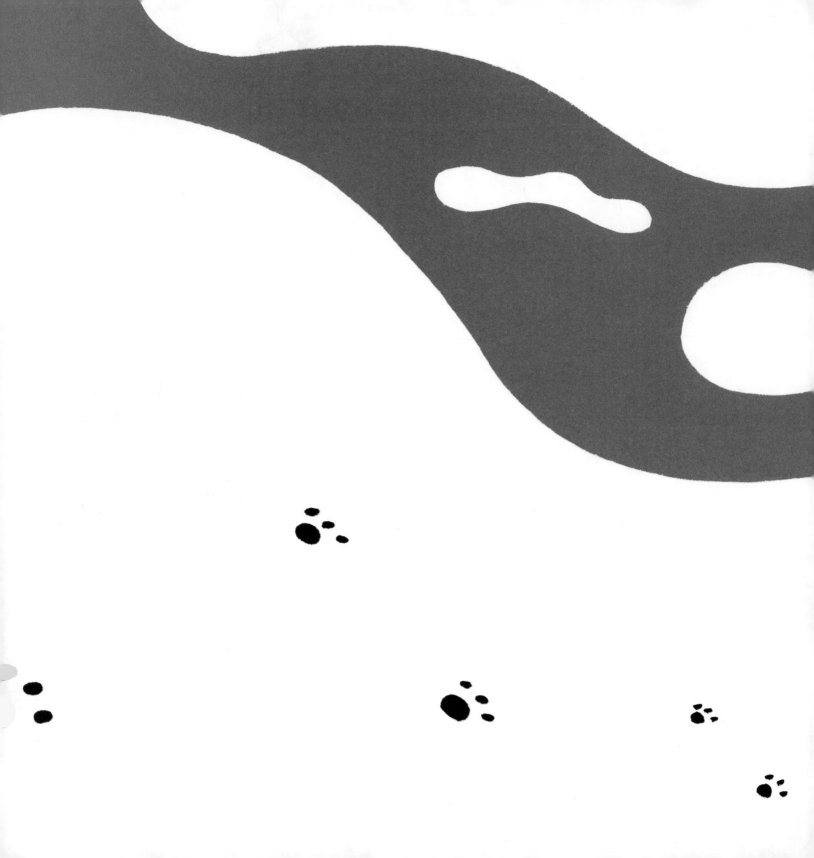